BOWL PATROL!

MARILYN JANOVITZ

NORTH-SOUTH BOOKS / NEW YORK / LONDON

TO TEASEL'S FRIEND DAVID

CAT

SCAT!

CHASE

RACE

SLURP

BURP!

STOP

DROP

HI!

BYE!

YAP

NAP

SIP

DIP

NO!

GO!

LEAP

DEEP

HOP

FLOP

CREEP

SLEEP?

SNEAK

PEEK

MORE?

SNORE

DRY

CRY

DARE

STARE

SHARE